xoxo to Papa, Dad, CharlieGramps, and CJZ.

– ED

To José and Vinicio; Vovô and Grandy. May all the long-distance grandfathers
in the world be able to visit and enjoy their grandchildren.

– LNP

As always, special thanks to KL & DW from ED & LNP

First Edition
Kane Miller, A Division of EDC Publishing

Text copyright © Erin Dealey 2018
Illustrations copyright © Luciana Navarro Powell 2018

www.kanemiller.com
www.edcpub.com
www.usbornebooksandmore.com

Library of Congress Control Number: 2016955632

Manufactured by Regent Publishing Services, Hong Kong
Printed March 2018 in ShenZhen, Guangdong, China

ISBN: 978-1-61067-616-8

1 2 3 4 5 6 7 8 9 10

Grandpa's Favorite

Written by Erin Dealey

Illustrated by Luciana Navarro Powell

Kane Miller
A DIVISION OF EDC PUBLISHING

My grandpa's favorite chair
rocks back and forth—yippee!
Like cowboys we go ridin'.
I gallop on his knee.

My grandpa's favorite cars
vroom around a track!

A hot dog smeared with mustard
is Grandpa's favorite snack.

My grandpa's favorite hat's
just right for peekaboo.

He likes to put it on
my head and whisper,
"Where are you?"

My grandpa scoops me off my feet
            to ride high on his shoulders.

His favorite place is anywhere
with surf, or snow, or boulders.

Our secret fishing hole
is Grandpa's favorite stream.

Sometimes he lets me bait the hook.
Sometimes we sit and dream.

My grandpa says his favorite naps
are any time of day.

I close my eyes and try to rest
while Grandpa snores away!

My grandpa's favorite club
has no meetings at all.

He carries his clubs in a bag
to hit a small white ball.

My grandpa's favorite sport
would be too hard to choose.

His favorite teams are on TV.
(He hates it when they lose!)

My grandpa's favorite truck
is at the fire station.
He used to drive the
hook and ladder.

Now he's on vacation.

My grandpa's favorite
tree keeps changing with
the weather.

Sometimes we pick the juicy fruit.
Sometimes we climb together.

My grandpa's favorite tools
can hammer, drill, and hack.

And when we finish fixing things,
I help him put them back.

My grandpa's favorite music
is never soft or quiet.

His favorite meal is anytime he isn't on a diet.

My grandpa likes to growl,
"I'm hungry as a bear!"
He makes my spoon into a plane
and flies it in the air.

My grandpa's favorite books
have heroes brave and true.
They save the earth, explore the world,
and someday I will too.

My grandpa says I make him proud
as any gramps can be.

And even when he's far away,

his favorite kid is ME!